Beckett at Greystones Bay

by Rosary Hartel O'Neill

SAMUEL FRENCH

FOUNDED 1830

NEW YORK HOLLYWOOD LONDON TORONTO

SAMUELFRENCH.COM

ISBN 978-0-573-69768-5   Printed in U.S.A.   #4255

MUSIC USE NOTE

IMPORTANT BILLING AND CREDIT
REQUIREMENTS

CHARACTERS

SAMUEL BECKETT— A writer, 27, smashing looking—tall and athletic, broad shoulders, angular features. Dishelveled clothes, grubby trousers, dirty raincoat several sizes too large on a thin frame, which has a text in one pocket and a bottle of stout in the other.

A CACOPHANY OF VOICES FROM HIS PAST: Loud, soft, haunting, brash:

> Brother's voice
>
> Father's voice
>
> Mother's voice
>
> Edna's voice
>
> Cousin Margaret's voice

SETTING

Greystones Bay, Ireland, winter 1933. Dusk. The coastline of Greystones is made of a large beach, rocky formations and a bay which hosts a small harbor. Sam's father is buried in a nearby cemetery.

ACT ONE

Scene 1

(The action takes place in the mind of **SAMUEL BECKETT** *with offstage voices from his past. These may be portrayed electronically or by actors. We're on a bleak stony beach. Winter. 1933. Dusk. Twilight shadows soak up the tattered sand.* **SAM** *limps in, carrying a pail with stones. His index finger is bandaged in gauze. He conveys an impression of elegance, though threadbare. His short reddish-brown hair is brushed to the right, revealing an aquiline nose, and haunting eyes. He has set up camp by a weather-worn chest. It contains bandage supplies, books, cigarettes, matches, and food. He faces the audience, responding to images of people he envisions in the sea. When he does so, faces appear on the rear scrim and/or actors representing these characters stand up in the audience. He yells out.)*

SAM. Go. I need to finish my book.

(Takes out a pencil and pad, writes. A whisper like a hoarse breeze. Lights dim. His **FATHER's** *image startles him.)*

SAM. Oh! Is that...you?

*(**SOUND:** Sound of breathing.)*

SAM. It can't be, but it is. Sit. Goodness. Well.

*(**SOUND:** Sound of breeze.)*

SAM. I'm glad to see you. You look good. Your hands aren't swollen any more. Did you come because they want to psychoanalyze me?

*(**SOUND:** An eerie rustling sound.)*

SAM. What's that? When I came back from your death bed, I felt completely lost. I crawled onto this beach and lay here for hours, like a husk. I don't know who I am or what I'm doing. I'm living a dying thing. You have already cut me loose, but I refuse to let you go. Bad move. Mother's lonely. Brother's getting married. Your dog, Wolf, died. Mother cried for two days....

FATHER. *(V.O.)* You must go.

SAM. You hated psychiatrists. If I can be out here in this place that you loved, I know my mind will clear up. I'll finish the book. Say something? Anything. *(**SOUND:** A low, barely perceptible heartbeat and shallow breathing.)*

FATHER. *(V.O.)* Go.

SAM. No.

*(**SOUND:** A clanging noise like a metal door closing. Ghost disappears.)*

SAM. Don't leave. Father.

(Fading wind. **SAM** *reaches toward the sky.)*

SAM. To quote Keats: "I have clung / To nothing, loved a nothing, nothing seen / Or felt but a great dream. O I have been / Presumptuous against love—"

*(**SAM** sees an image of his **BROTHER**. Screech of seagulls.)*

BROTHER. *(V.O.)* See the psychiatrist.

SAM. Oh, Brother. I can't. When you write on the beach, its majesty gives you hope. It hits the eye with possibilities. You'll find more crazy people inland where they are not challenged. *(Breathes heavily.)* I don't speak much, but I can to prove my sanity.

FATHER *(V.O.)* Fight, fight, fight, and when you're tired fight some more.

SAM. That's what Father said. He was strapped to the bed because even after that massive coronary, he tried to pull himself out. Father said I was a star and—

*(**SOUND:** Murmur of word "star" echoes on the breeze.)*

SAM. "Everyone wants to shoot a star. Pow. Pow. Pow." But Father said—

SAM and **FATHER** *(V.O.)* What you don't have, you don't need.

(Sound of "need" on the wind. **SAM** *rummages for a match. To* **BROTHER**.*)*

SAM. Smoking stiffens my courage. Other times I whistle. *(Takes out a tin whistle. Demonstrates.)* I'm a writer, for God's sake. I can't let them burn that out of me. One day my name may mean something. Now it doesn't mean I need a big-city psychiatrist. Those people are outlawed in this country. That's right.

They're forbidden to practice here. *(Angrily.)* You try to change someone; it's a big blow to his soul. I'm not sick. Artists work in solitary confinement because we fear people are completely mad. Course we could be crazy. *(Laughs.)* Time for a joke. A writer lived with his publicist until she quit doing publicity. Said *(cont.)* she was tired of being number two. "No," he said. "My writing is number one, I'm number two, and you're number three."

BROTHER. *(V.O.)* Come inside.

SAM. As you distance yourself, you see family as intrusions. Great artists have all proven to have deformities of their psychological profiles. Writers are powerful people, not group-oriented husks. A book may be beautiful but it's also gratification for control. I'm the heir to Dante, Proust, Shakespeare.

(Doubles over with a stomach cramp.)

BROTHER. *(V.O.)* You're sick.

SAM. True, I sleep with you to stop my panic, but it stops. *(Breathes quickly as if suffocating.)* Arrogance—keeps me writing through a chain of failures.

BROTHER. *(V.O.)* It's a shallow existence.

SAM. No, it's defiant. The world is watching writers. The world needs hope. The homeless need us. The hungry need us. Those in prison need us. Our calling is high and holy. *(Pause.)* What is the universe asking you to give up to follow your path? *(Pause.)* Nothing? No one's called to the easy life. Nevertheless— "There never lived a mortal man, who bent / His appetite beyond his natural sphere / But starved and died." John Keats, my mentor, died in glory at 26.

BROTHER. *(V.O.)* Stop those thoughts.

SAM. The mind's natural prey is itself. *(Takes books out of the chest.)* I take satisfaction from organizing my books. These baby steps give me pinpricks of joy. I always carry a book. It's my cross against life's vampires. *(Lifts book against the sky, paces.)* I can hold up the book and say stay away because this is the power I have. Every artwork is a prayer. The authentic poem, picture, song, they're prayers releasing hope in the onlooker like the response to a psalm. Priest: The word of the Lord. Respondent: Thanks be to God. Language lifts my soul. Words and I saved each other.

SAM. "When by my solitary heart I sit, / And hateful thoughts enwrap my soul in gloom: / Sweet Hope, ethereal balm upon me shed—"

(**SOUND:** *Rattle of breeze*)

SAM. *(To* **BROTHER***)Mother* doesn't like Keats—well, no matter. It takes a lot to kill my enthusiasm.

(**SAM** *grinds cigarette, chews it, rummages for a match.*)

MOTHER. *(V.O.)* Your suffering is mental, son.

SAM. Night sweats, shudders, breathlessness...*(Gasps for air.)* even total paralysis, it's make-believe.

MOTHER. *(V.O.)* You should teach.

SAM. Colleagues wheeze by to have a look, offer me a yawner course. I don't want to talk to stupid people. You have to work too hard. I resigned because, because...not because I was ill. *(Catching his breath.)* I need to be around brave people. *(Gasps.)* These students, they're tombstones. Nondescript. *(Feeling an abdominal pain.)* What could be more violent than killing a part of myself for money? I have to numb myself to that ambition that propelled me through all those years of intensity. If I'm going to do that I'll put a gun to my head and shoot it. *(Grabs his chest as if having palpitations.)* Yes, Mother. I apologize. I don't want life to be about minor disputes. I took the job, didn't I? Once they had me, they bloody screwed me. There was such hatred of high standards; I walked through the campus like a target.

(**SOUND:** *Indecipherable murmurings.*)

SAM. These men talk more than they think. Tiny thoughts after each huge diatribe.

(**SOUND:** *A crescendo of mumbling.*)

SAM. I'm too overqualified. I don't mean that egotistically. I mean that factually. *(Pause.)* I'm a book on the shelf, insurance for the rare student.

MOTHER. *(V.O.)* Don't flatter yourself.

SAM. *(To* **MOTHER***)* If I give teaching time to writing—I could create something superior. "Every deep-thinking mind tries to clarify thought. This is only perfectly attained in writing."

*(A clawing wind. He tightens the jacket about him. **BROTHER**'s image reappears. To **BROTHER**.)*

SAM. I don't blame Mother. To always think alone, it hardens you. *(He gives up on the cigarette and tosses it.)* I'm not compulsive. For months, the only joy I had was my writing and part of me craves that. *(Pause.)* At some point, an artist is no longer a part of the university team, a member of the family, a half of a couple. You are ostracized or you self-ostracize. *(Pause.)* Writing became my safe *(cont.)* harbor. Paper would receive my tears. Paper would hold all for me till I could figure it out. *(Pause.)* But I gave my soul to a cause that evaporated. All my writer friends stripped off their veneer and put on a suit and tie. *(Tightens fist.)* God, my finger hurts. *(Punches the air.)*

BROTHER. *(V.O.)* You were the heavyweight champion of school.

SAM. Some things can't be fixed. If you're a psycho, they can't fix you. *(Pause.)* Time for a laugh. A minister told his congregation, "Next week I plan to preach about the sin of lying. To help you understand my sermon, I want you all to read Mark 17." The following Sunday as he prepared to deliver his sermon, the minister asked for a show of hands. He wanted to know how many had read Mark 17. Every hand went up. The minister smiled and said, "Mark has only 16 chapters. I will now proceed with my sermon on the sin of lying."

*(**SAM** unwraps gauze and tends to a festering boil.)*

SAM. The suffering of the skin is the caustic encrustation of feelings defied. I have to inspect my body every day for ticks, for toxicity.

BROTHER. *(V.O.)* Get straightened out and you'll write again.

SAM. I haven't stopped writing. I've got a lot of attention out of being ill, so I'm always going to be doing that. *(A cold breeze. He blows on his numb fingertips. Removes a shrimp shell.)* I studied whether a crustacean can suffer in my last story. I gave Mother three copies. *(Pause. Laughs.)* Not shells, books. No, I don't want my writing to offend. I'm not mocking anyone.

(He unwinds long strips of gauze which drift in the breeze.)

BROTHER. *(V.O.)* See the psychiatrist.

SAM. Back, Brother! You're in my light. My neck's oozing, my foot's purple, I think I'm bloody dead. I even have a—bump on my bottom. I can't sit long. But I can write standing up. *(He exposes finger, neck, and foot wounds.)* Disappointing? I know.

BROTHER. *(V.O.)* All through life you kept in shape.

SAM. Golf is still what I'm best at. Golf is not a team sport, like publishing. There's one person standing at that tee, one person lifting that club. When I swing, I imagine I'm powerful like Schopenhauer, the great pessimist. *(SAM puts a shell over his nose, changes his voice.)* He said, "Art is not like science, merely concerned with reasoning, but with one's soul. Each must count for what he is in reality." Schopenhauer—who received a reply that most of his first *(cont.)* publication had been disposed of as waste paper. Later when I lance all my boils, I'll pretend I'm Keats, moving toward beauty. "Beauty is truth, truth beauty—" Surely you know that. I don't just collect quotes. I memorize books. Keats goes deep into depression, and that makes me feel better. "I have been in love with easeful Death, / Called him soft names in many a mused rhyme, / To take into the air my quiet breath—" *(Pause)* There's been a rupture of everyone I was close to. Not you, no.

(He blots a boil. Takes out a razor and fresh gauze.)

BROTHER. *(V.O.)* Mother's worried.

SAM. Yes, I've read Mother's daily notes, her copies of the "Times," with her exhortations that I might earn money by writing for the obituary section. I'm not running from responsibility. I washed and shaved Father after his coronaries, even though he found it intolerable and started to cry. I changed the bedpans, and drove Mother to the hospital. *(He blots another boil.)* In our family, she gets to hold the leash. She's the rigid one. I'm not. Oh no. This weepiness is humiliating. This panic-stricken stasis of Keats, crouched in a mossy thicket annulled, like a bee in sweetness, drowned with the fumes of poppies. *(Begins to lance finger.)* It's okay to cry as a purging tool like a spring rain. Ooh.

BROTHER. *(V.O.)* You want a pill?

SAM. No! How much rest do we need to make up for a loss?

BROTHER. *(V.O.)* A blanket?

SAM. I'm not cold. Smile, Brother. Only friends I want are...those who are profoundly happy.

BROTHER. *(V.O.)* Fresh bandages?

SAM. Not so close. I realize there are absences I've had for years and I'd made no progress in reducing them even though I'd read and thought a great deal.

(SAM lifts a stone to the light.)

SAM. Look at that? Here, I'm back. Part of me that was empty is full again. I want to wake up every morning watching the breeze shimmering over stones. My eyes drift deep into the gray greens. I distract myself by counting the colors: the amber tans, pearl blues, gray browns. I'm falling in love with stones.

(SAM wanders off alone, stares out to sea. Tide laps in and out.)

SAM. I take stones home; lay them into the branches of trees. It's a pre-birth nostalgia to return to the mineral state...to an untouched spring that hasn't been contaminated. When I walk through a stony landscape I study the grays, the different contours. You can be in hell among the stones and still be happy. *(Picks up stones.)*

BROTHER. *(V.O.)* Come back.

SAM. I don't want to go inside, feel a loss of beauty. Be exposed to the illogical cowardly things that go on in there. The house never was mine. It will go like the tide sliding over stones. When I look at their silver sheen, I feel peace. I'm in touch with God when I'm here.

SOUND: Wave sounds rip the water. Distant hum of a motor boat.

SAM. Father loved little boats. Once we were out on rough waves and I panicked and he crawled over and slapped me. And I calmed down because Father never hit us.

(SAM collects stones.)

(SOUND: Distant song from the church, like, "I will raise him up. I will raise him up. I will raise him up on the last day.")

SAM. Another dirge from Saint Mary's. The man died of a heart attack. There's one more *Mater Dolorosa.*

BROTHER. *(V.O.)* Ma wants you to be a pallbearer.

SAM. I don't like being around concentrations of people. I have to be so vigilant; I consider it a waste of time. "The dark impression of that Nothing, which we fear like children, the darkness." Schopenhauer. How can I lift the casket, walk in the church, the man I knew so well, gone with no way of changing that? I'm not going to make choices, which are not in my interest. I choose to live in a gray world of low extremities.

BROTHER. *(V.O.)* Be a pallbearer.

SAM. Hang around the casket. Watch the lid close. Click. I can't walk behind the hearse.

(SOUND: Sound of tolling church bells.)

SAM. *(Recites)* "Where are the songs of spring? Aw where are they? / Think not of them, thou hast thy music too,— / While barred clouds, bloom the soft-dying day."

(SOUND: Gulls caw.)

SAM. *(To BROTHER)* When the house sells, I want only the piano and the green settee.

(Looks up, sees his father.)

SAM. *(To FATHER)* Father, you needn't come home? In full regalia, hat, coat, polished shoes, I don't have high fever. You don't have to keep me in place, sit by, and tell a story.

(Ghost vanishes.)

SAM. Now that's the task of the radio, the record player. The role of the storyteller has evaporated.

(SOUND: Tide laps out.)

BROTHER. *(V.O.)* Treatment is the only hope.

SAM. I can't submit. It'll kill my inspiration.

BROTHER. *(V.O.)* It'll unleash your artistic force.

SAM. Sometimes I taste the excitement of being free. Other times...

MOTHER. *(V.O.)* You're selfish, a hypochondriac.

SAM. *(To* **BROTHER.***)* In my family my illness is a fantasy. *(Pause.)* I'm not angry, Brother. But I keep having to forgive the same people and that's hard, because every time I forgive them, they do another nasty thing to me. *(Rewraps finger.)* Not you, Brother. Mother. The town. It's never been a city that—. My stories always get axed. I'm too much a part of here to be considered anything special. People who don't write don't know the challenge to remain stable *(cont.)* in a world that rejects what you do. When I see a publisher, I put on a face. *(Pause.)* I like reading in waiting rooms. I've got 15 different books I study about art, philosophy, psychology. I survive because I'm tenacious. *(Chuckles.)* No, that's not part of my control thing. If publishers think you're marshmallow, they'll shoot their whole quiver into you.

BROTHER. *(V.O.)* Relax.

SAM. How can your work be valuable when everyone wants to rewrite it? You have to be vigilant. Let these cowards know that if they muck up your book, they're going to die. And let the cowards move on. Sometimes I don't want to do that... *(Looks up, points.)* like that bird that chased the others off. He held his ground. But human beings shouldn't have to act like buzzards. Oh yeah, it's OK, scrap me again. I'm fine. *(Winces.)* Ooh. I've got to lance this finger.

BROTHER. *(V.O.)* Rest.

SAM. Sometimes I think of how it might be if I could sit back and smile at my life instead of having to rewrap a boil. *(Laughs.)*

(SOUND: Tolling church bells.)

SAM. *(To* **BROTHER.***)* Do I like sex? I am what you'd call a randy individual. R-A-N-D-Y. I don't like sex, I love it. Brothels, dirty books...everything. Ecstasy organs do give joy, but...chasing physical traits can lead you on the road to ruin. The crossroads for me was when I had perverts wanting to have sex with me. *(Laughs.)* After a while, lust goes away. Our main job is to reproduce, which I failed at. "But put therein some drug designed / To banish woman from my mind."

BROTHER. *(V.O.)* Why not quote yourself?

SAM. Because Keats found an audience. *(Pause. Laughs.)* It's not inadequacy. I don't have to look up; I can look even with Keats. He was luckier, more focused. *(Pause.)* And yes, I would like a woman in my life.

*(**SOUND:** "Ave Maria" peals from the church.)*

*(**SAM** collects stones.)*

SAM. Any intellectual realizes another deeply-connected human being cushions you against adversity. It's like yeah, I could march into this battle alone, but if you stood with me, it'd be easier. As an artist, you look obsessively for a mate because you're so unmatched in every other area. I'd like someone who likes *(cont.)* silence, nature, touch—but I can get by with a more peripheral relationship. I don't need constant interaction. Just...the promise. I was hoping I didn't have to work...that my dream woman would come to me.

BROTHER. *(V.O.)* You pick girls you can't have.

SAM. You're either going to get stung by women or your conscience will sting you cause you're alone.

BROTHER. *(V.O.)* You held out till college.

SAM. True. Before, I always looked away. My excuse was, "They aren't good enough for me." But I wasn't ready to bare my soul. "Dark violet eyes; Soft dimpled hands, white neck, and creamy breast—"

BROTHER. *(V.O.)* Edna.

SAM. I held back love for so long, when Edna came before me, I couldn't stop my dazzled senses.

BROTHER. *(V.O.)* What a beauty.

SAM. We met twice that first day, exchanging general, then more intimate views, and I considered this significant. I got hooked on the fantasy—for weeks the most important thing was the words we shared.

*To **EDNA**.)* You like novels, Edna? We could read Proust together.

EDNA. *(V.O.)* Marvelous.

EDNA *(V.O.)* and **SAM.** "For a long time, I used to go to bed early. Sometimes when I had put out my candle, my eyes would close so quickly that—"

SAM. *(To* **EDNA***)* You want to meet each day to read? Yes, oh yes.

SAM and **ENDA.** *(V.O.)* "When a man is asleep, he has in a circle round him the chain of the hours, the sequence of the years, the order of the heavenly host."

BROTHER. Don't go back there.

(SOUND: The cackling of sea gulls.)

(SAM scoops up pebbles. Hurls a stone. To **BROTHER***.)*

SAM. Edna was living a life completely unknown to me, but I basked in the drivel of time I was given. Edna was not talkative, so I envisioned her profound; she was depressed, so I imagined her deep; sarcastic, so I found her witty. I didn't realize cruelty had seeped into her behavior. When we finally kissed, I became subsumed in her.

BROTHER. *(V.O.)* Don't torture yourself.

SAM. She disappeared with my best friend to the country. Did they have sex? She and he knew each other before. *(Pause.)* For years, he and I were close, but soon as he got the chance—I don't want to go through life with a grudge, but people are astonishing. *(Pause.)* After that one trip Edna didn't want to see me again.

EDNA. *(V.O.)* I can't give you more than 15 minutes a day.

SAM. When you fasten onto a wild horse, you should know how to ride it. I don't want to degrade her. She's not here to defend herself. "Only man causes pain without any further object than doing so. No animal ever tortures for the sake of torturing." *(Chuckles.)* What about cats? Don't they torment their prey? *(Laughs.)* Only psychotic cats that've been civilized do that.

SOUND: Screeching of a wild bird.

SAM. Edna married him. And only Keats was there. "He did not rave, he did not stare aghast, / For all those visions were o'ergone, and past—"

BROTHER. *(V.O.)* Ninety percent of women will steal your soul.

SAM. Yes. It's in their genes to do that. I don't blame her. I've a dangerous tendency to fantasize. It probably comes from all the alcohol I took when I was younger....The books I read are clarifying meaning comes from what I give to the outside world. That truly bothers me.

(SOUND: Wind rises, blowing papers about.)

SAM. *(Laughs nervously.)* Perhaps I should move to a big city. Egg and bacon dripping on a counter, cigarette butts gumming the floor. Find safety in anonymity.

BROTHER. *(V.O.)* It's a cruel craft.

SAM. Joke time: Three little boys were concerned because they couldn't get anyone to play with them. They decided it was because they hadn't been baptized and didn't go to Sunday school. So they went to the nearest church. Only the janitor was there. One said, "Nobody will play with us. Won't you baptize us?" "Sure," said the janitor. He took them into the bathroom and dunked their heads in the toilet bowl, one at a time. Then he said, "Now go out and play." When they got outside, dripping wet, one of them asked, "What religion are we?" The oldest said, "We're not Katlick, because they pour water on you. We're not Baplist because they dunk all of you." The littlest said, "Didn't you smell that water?" "Yes. What do you think that means?" "That means we're Pisscopalians."

(SOUND: Bells toll in the distance.)

SAM. *(To* **BROTHER***)* Father's house and the beach, this was our world. *(Smiles, shirks off the wind.)* I glimpse flashes of us. I saw a boy on the beach, the image of you, and I realized, no, you're grown up. And I spotted this man playing ball and God, he looked like Father.

(SOUND: The bells toll louder.)

SAM. "Ask not for whom the bell tolls. It tolls for thee." *(Looks at the sky.)* Why was I set adrift?

BROTHER. *(V.O.)* Don't think so much.

FATHER *(V.O.)* You don't work with your brains, you'll work with your back.

SAM. Father was a silent partner. He didn't need long discussions. He loved life. *(Lifts up a piece of cardboard.)* I kept the sign he put by his hospital bed. "Don't quit." Father could determine health by looking into our eyes. Talking to him was a validation I was sane. *(Pause.)* His last words were:

SAM and **FATHER V.O.** I'm proud of you getting that professor's post.

(SOUND: Tolling bells fade into the sea.)

SAM. *(To* **MOTHER.***)* I don't want a tea biscuit or cheese. Food pours in, while the appetite stops. *(Laughs. Cautiously.)* Thanks for the basket, Mother. I'm sorry you had to go...to your room. *(Chuckles.)* No, I'm not disputing why. *(Pause.)* Yes, I'll give you my full attention. I'll put down the pencil. No, I admire your facing issues. Say something. We don't live in a telepathic world—

MOTHER. *(V.O.)* You're self-absorbed.

SAM. I feel bad I'm not with you, but Brother's there. I'd like to give you what you want: money, grandchildren. But I can't rise at five to write before I drive you about. I avoid taking lunch so I won't get sidetracked in the kitchen. *(Angrily.)* Maybe you should get a dog, some furry creature to chase you. Sorry. Don't cry. *(Pause.)*Don't. I wish I hadn't said that. Before we were all so damn responsible, people didn't expect so much. I like to please you, but...You keep trying to fashion me into something that works for you, not me. *(Pause.)* I can't...come home. We choose a path because it seems easier at the time, and the time becomes the life.

MOTHER. *(V.O.)* You're an egomaniac.

SAM. *(Paces angrily.)* Did throwing my books out make you happy? I can't live in jolly discomfort, putting aside my "fancy dreams." Cling to every cent as if it could save me. *(Pause.)* Now you're giving me the silent treatment. I, well, I won't sanctify money. I'll dope, numb or kill myself—first. *(Pause.)* Eventually I'm going to be gone from here because soon these books won't be enough. *(Pause.)* Don't walk away, Mother. Don't leave while I'm speaking. I've a sore throat. *(Pause.)* Mother.

MOTHER. *(V.O.)* Vile. Filth.

SAM. *(To* **MOTHER***)* I won't stop. How dare I ponder new ideas when you're stuck in repetition?

MOTHER. *(V.O.)* You said you'd make time for me.

SAM. You dump my books in the trash.

BROTHER. *(V.O.)* Leave her be.

SAM. *(To* **BROTHER***)* It's confusing when the bad people become good, and the good people become bad. She's shown nothing but hatred for my calling. Tardiness with messages. Hiding mail. Throwing my writing out.

BROTHER. *(V.O.)* Calm down. Come inside.

SAM. I don't want to see that house. I want to remember it when Father was there. Home was Father, more than anything else. "Turning and turning in the widening gyre / The falcon cannot hear the falconer, / Things fall apart, the center cannot hold. / More anarchy is tossed upon the world."

(Screeching of seagulls. **SAM** *is suddenly paralyzed. He screams.)*

SAM. Oh God.

SAM. *(To* **BROTHER***)* I'm afraid to move. I'd like to plan my life, but there's intransigence now. I'm in the synapse, the gap between. "Midway along the journey of our life, / I woke to find myself in some dark woods, / For I had wandered off from the straight path." *(Pause)* Don't touch. I need a suicide specialist. Some potion to release the soul. *(Pause)* Paris is a place that calls me. In Paris, I perceive my path as normal. You can find this enclave of writers who've chosen to make the sacrifices necessary to grow. *(Pause)* Maybe writing attracts people with a gene for insanity? Does manic depression birth literary creativity? If to survive, an artist has to put up with insecurity, neglect, ridicule, he will show the psychic effect of adverse conditions. In 1550, young Italian artists *(cont.)* displayed savagery and madness, while in the Egyptian civilization or the Middle Ages, artists were pleasant and well adjusted.

FATHER. *(V.O.)* Suffering can be a challenge.

SAM. I think if I keep questioning a door will eventually open and someone will say, "I know you've been knocking for a long time; I'd like to let you in."

FATHER. *(V.O.)* Writers are soothsayers paving the way.

SAM. "But educated people draw little distinction between the trade of a poet or that of an embroiderer." If I put all my personal soul in my work, people will see me as an alien. *(Pause)* Another joke? A couple, age 76, went to the doctor's office. The doctor asked, "What can I do for you?" The man said, "Will you watch us have sexual intercourse?" The doctor looked puzzled but agreed. When

18

the couple had finished, the doctor said, "There's nothing wrong with the way you have intercourse," and charged them $10. This happened several weeks in a row. The couple would make an appointment, have intercourse, pay the doctor and leave. Finally the doctor asked, "What exactly are you trying to find out?" The old man said, "We're not trying to find out anything. She is married and we can't go to her house. I'm married and we can't go to my house. The Inn charges $30. We do it here for $10 and get back $8 from the government for a doctor's visit."

*(**SOUND:** A woman's breathing and laughing.)*

MARGARET. *(V.O.)* Perhaps laughter releases the soul.

FATHER. *(V.O.)* Come along.

*(**SAM** looks up, shocked.)*

SAM. Father. Oh my God. It's Father and Cousin Margaret.

MARGARET. *(V.O.)* Help! Help.

SAM. Where are you, Margaret? I can't see. Don't go. I can't find you. You're fading.

*(**SOUND:** Sound of woman breathing.)*

SAM. Come back. I miss the sweetness of your body. Come back. I need your soft embrace.

BROTHER. *(V.O.)* Don't think about her.

SAM. I must. Cousin Margaret!

*(**SOUND:** Echoing of "Cousin Margaret" on the breeze. Her laughter.)*

SAM. "Come live with me and be my love, / And we will some new pleasures prove—"

MARGARET. *(V.O.)* What do you like best about me?

SAM. The names you call me...

MARGARET. *(Overlapping)* Dear, dearest, precious.

SAM. What else?

MARGARET. *(V.O.)* Your brilliant naiveté which comes from living in the world of dreams.

SAM. With you, "I would be ignorant as the dawn—" I dreamed I can fly and I do. I can fly. I'd forgotten that. Up with a thought and quickly I'm off with these amazing powers—. I am a bird, flying up. I don't worry. I'm free. I land anywhere. I'm free.

(SOUND: Cousin Margaret breathing.)

SAM. My favorite thing is to watch you. You're beautiful, and even more intelligent. I'd be happy being engaged for a long time. I want us always to be touching. Everyone needs a guardian angel. When I walk into any crisis, I call forth how you would handle it. "Who can doubt whether we are in the world for anything but love?"

(SOUND: A heartbeat.)

BROTHER. *(V.O.)* You're obsessed.

SAM. Margaret carries my picture around and kisses the lips. She needs affection every day like people need food.

MARGARET. *(Eerily, from a distance)* Do you love me as much as the first day we kissed?

SAM. *(To MARGARET)* Sure. Some couples don't set dates when they get engaged. I...I can't commit now.

MOTHER. *(V.O.)* She is using you, son.

SAM. I know she cares. With Margaret, I've given up hopelessness.

MOTHER. *(V.O.)* It's a trap.

SAM. I know your limitations. I don't expect you to be thoughtful. Margaret wants me to live free as a bird. *(Pause.)* I've decided to marry her.

MOTHER. *(V.O.)* First cousins can't marry.

SAM. I knew you'd make me feel bad. I've my feet parked firmly and I'm holding to my course.

MOTHER. *(V.O.)* It's forbidden by the medical profession, the Church.

SAM. We won't have children.

MOTHER. *(V.O.)* See someone else.

SAM. I won't let her go, back off from...from planning the future. When Margaret thought I'd stopped loving her, her eyes went red and she told everyone she had a fever. I said, "Don't listen to Mother."

MOTHER. *(V.O.)* I wish Margaret loved you like I loved your father.

SAM. *(Angrily, to* **MARGARET***)* Quiet.

*(**SOUND**: The Angelus drones in the distance.)*

SAM. *(To* **MARGARET***)* I walk about in circles. The point is not whether we marry, but we are growing apart.

MARGARET. *(V.O.)* Sometimes I miss you. Sometimes I don't.

SAM. *(To* **MARGARET***.)* I don't know what Mother said to your parents, but you can't cut me off. *(To* **BROTHER***.)* We showed Mother Margaret's ring. I said, "Mother, we're engaged." Mother looked away and said, "So what." I couldn't confront Mother. So Mother ignored Margaret. When Margaret said your mother has a mean streak, I defended her. "She loves her sons," I said. "She did worse to Brother's wife. Talk to her."

MARGARET. *(V.O.)* You choose your mother over me.

SAM. "The ceremony of innocence is drowned; / The best lack all conviction, while the worst / Are full of passionate intensity." *(To* **BROTHER***)* I suppose if we had a definite wedding date, Mother's cruelty wouldn't bother Margaret.

MARGARET. *(V.O.)* She's perfected unkindness.

SAM. *(To* **MARGARET***)* Mother's taken a fall. I can't upset her.

MARGARET. *(V.O.)* She acts like a wife, making you hold her hand, sit by her.

SAM. *(To* **BROTHER.***)* Margaret fears we'll have to live far away.

MARGARET. *(V.O.)* She began removing her clothes in front of you—

SAM. Mother comes from a big family. She had that weak spell.

MARGARET. *(V.O.)* But even so, pulling up her nightgown to show you where she fell.

SAM. I looked away.

MARGARET. *(V.O.)* Wanting you to change her lingerie.

SAM. I can't get involved in all this. I can't be forthright. So little time with you and you won't—

SAM. *(To* **BROTHER.***)* Cousin Margaret says no matter what she does, even if she sees her priest daily, she can't overcome her anxiety. I can't bear not seeing her. She won't elope. "It is asked whether it is necessary to love. This should not be asked, it should be felt. We do not deliberate upon it, we are forced to it."

MARGARET. *(V.O.)* There's an intimacy you won't share with me.

SAM. *(To* **MARGARET.***)* Now you just wish to meditate and sit in the garden. What do you want me to do exactly? Disappear from your life?

MARGARET. *(V.O.)* My plants bloom for me as if they're my children.

SAM. *(To* **MARGARET.***)* We're doing a tango. One step forward, two steps back.

MARGARET. *(V.O.)* I'm happy to putter here—

SAM. *(To* **MARGARET.***)* And not talk. I don't want to marry someone uncertain. But— No, I won't take back the ring.

MARGARET. *(V.O.)* It doesn't mean we're engaged. There's no date.

SAM. Wear it on your middle finger.

BROTHER. *(V.O.)* Her leaving was a brave gift because there would have been an explosion.

SAM. *(To* **MARGARET.***)* I reread your letter: "In order to honor our past relationship, you—"

SAM and **MARGARET** *(V.O.).* Release me from our engagement vows, and hope blessings will come my way."

SAM. *(To* **MARGARET.***)* On what grounds are you leaving me? "What the hammer? What the chain? / In what furnace was the brain? / What the anvil? What dread grasp / Dare its deadly terrors clasp?"

(SOUND: Sound of erratic heartbeat.)

BROTHER. *(V.O.)* Margaret's a high fever.

SAM. What? No . . .when?

MARGARET. *(V.O.)* No safe haven till I meet God.

BROTHER. *(V.O.)* A severe infection. It came on sudden, quick.

SAM. *(To* **BROTHER.***)* Oh God. Hold on. I'm coming. Nothing will separate us. Hold on! Heartbeat irregular, fading... Margaret's arms are weeping from the injections. She can't eat because of the tubes down her throat. She is letting go of her old body. Sores all over her hands. When I asked her to let me know if she knew me, she made a violent gasp. Brother says often she is in another place outside her body. Margaret rallied, then failed. She doesn't want to get out of bed. First they decline badly and then they dive. They are letting Margaret die, weaning her off food, then her other systems will shut down. *(Pause)* "Suddenly I saw the cold and rook-delighting heaven, / But that seemed as though ice burned and was but the more ice." *(Pause)* Margaret can't squeeze my hand or say anything. *(Pause.)* She died. I stay in the present, and by doing so, I don't cry. Margaret was half there in her shell body. We are 98% energy. But now her 2% is gone.

SOUND: A funeral bell tolls.

SAM. I still wake up wanting to hold her. *(Looks around.)* There are hyacinths all over. She looks cold but peaceful. There's the sunshine dress from her mother. So fluffed, ribbed cotton.

BROTHER. *(V.O.)* We should leave.

SAM. I like being in the same room as Margaret. Feel if I stand by, I can protect her. Look at the hand-embroidered pictures of the beatitudes overhead. Her face looks old. Her color is yellow. Couldn't they do something about that? Her hands are covered with a handkerchief; they are so discolored.

BROTHER. *(V.O.)* Her body is there but not her soul.

SAM. Maybe my body is here, but not my soul.

MOTHER. *(V.O.)* No one dies of a broken heart.

SAM. "Through me the way into the doleful city, Through me the way into eternal grief, through me the way among a race forsaken. Abandon hope forever you who enter."

(SAM starts to drink.)

SAM. *(To* **BROTHER.***)* I take whiskey to get out of my brain, which would eat me, alive. "Man is but a reed, the feeblest thing in nature...A vapor, a drop of water suffice to kill him." I came far in my desire for intimacy, but I didn't make the final hurdle. Margaret abandoned me, and that's what I thought I was going to do. *(Pause.)* Death stalks us and wins. Joke time. "That was a terrible storm ye had down your way." "Twas surely. Our hen had her back to the wind and she laid the same egg five times." Or, "A ghost in the town of macroon, / One night found a ghoul in his room / They argued all night, as to which had the right, / To frighten the wits out of whom."

BROTHER. *(V.O.)* Don't blame yourself—

SAM. I don't have to think of worst-case scenarios, they're here.

(Billowy scrim, vague faces, soft light, misty.)

(SOUND: All voices cry, "Come inside.")

(SAM away, looks deep into the sea.)

SAM. "I live my life in widening rings, which spread over earth and sky." *(To* **MOTHER.***)* There's a balance between how much insult you're willing to take and how much you're willing to protect your feelings. *(Pause.)* My major debate is when to put the pillow over your head. *(Laughs.)*

MOTHER. Don't start with your poor me.

SAM. I see more than you. I've been to the extremity of experience. Been on the edge. Don't grab your head. You're not dying. What did you tell Margaret? What? Viper...No, I will not shut up. Pretending you need me while draining my life. No, I'll not be quiet. I'll scream and rage. Better yet, I'll slit my wrists in front of you. Lance a finger. Cut an eye out. You killed Margaret by turning me into a coward. A weepy Keats crouched in a thicket. Well, no more. I'll cut the umbilical cord. Pry my way out.

(Begins to pack.)

SAM. *(To* **BROTHER.***)* I'm leaving for London, psychoanalysis, hospitalization, who cares what. If Mother's in a rage, I'll leave the range of fire. *(Pause.)* Was a time when the thought of going would have sent me into a frenzy.

MOTHER. *(V.O.) (calls out)* Don't leave.

SAM. Now terror inspires me. Then again, maybe I'll get on the train and come right back.

MOTHER. *(Cries)* We need you.

SAM. *(To* **MOTHER.***)* I suckled at the tits of wolves and emerged with my humanity intact. Their behavior has contaminated me—

MOTHER. *(V.O.)* Oh, son. Don't scream.

SAM. You're not on anyone's side. You exist for yourself. You know I'll drive a stake through your heart if you fuck with me. You've the nervous system of a rattlesnake. Drop you off naked in Antarctica, you'll survive.

MOTHER. *(V.O.)* Don't be angry, son.

SAM. If I don't do what's right, what you want me to do, will I set something off?

MOTHER. *(V.O.)* You know I love you.

SAM. You think this is the greatest place because you live here. In our family you get to hold the leash. I've got rid of so much I feel like I'm a dead person.

MOTHER. *(V.O.)* This is your home, son.

SAM. No, it's not. It's a big house to have nobody in.

MOTHER. *(V.O.)* You're breaking my heart.

SAM. The older I get, the easier it is to do things that are devastating. Every place I go there's something wrong with me. I've got to start getting used to living in my own chaos.

MOTHER. *(V.O.)* Sit by me.

SAM. I knew at 9 years old that I'd never have the answers to your questions. I remember looking in the mirror saying, "You will never have the answers to her questions." So I comforted myself with Pascal's *Pensées*. "How happy is a life that begins with love and ends with ambition!"

MOTHER. *(V.O.)* Hold your mother's hand.

BROTHER. *(V.O.)* You're making Mother cry.

SAM. No. I just realized it's over for you, Brother, and me. Eventually it all goes away anyway. It's not if I leave, it's when. *(Pause.)* I'll move to Paris. Whenever I go to Paris, I feel loved. I guess the key is to leave, not to wait.

*(**SOUND:** Wind rises. Voices call out: "Stay! Stay!")*

SAM. So long, beach and sky. So long, wind and greystones—Father and— Margaret, Brother—forgive me.

*(A whisper like a hoarse breeze. Lights dim. His **FATHER**'s image startles him.)*

SAM. When the going gets rough, I want to yell, "Father." Should I go to the hospital? Get psychoanalyzed. I don't know. That's as close to a yes as I'm going to get. You don't have to be sick to die. I'll keep moving forward. And I'll keep my feet gripping for the next hold on the rock edge. If I do this religiously, nothing but stars await me now. *(Pause)* Maybe the heavens will open up and swallow me. "Rest not! Life is sweeping by; / Go and dare before you die. / Something mighty and sublime, / Leave behind to conquer time."

(curtain)

Also by
Rosary Hartel O'Neill...

The Awakening of Kate Chopin
Black Jack: The Thief of Possession
Degas in New Orleans
John Singer Sargent and Madame X
A Louisiana Gentleman
Marilyn/God
Property
Solitaire
Trutle Soup
Uncle Victor
White Suits in Summer
The Wings of Madness
Wishing Aces

Please visit our website **samuelfrench.com** for complete
descriptions and licensing information.